P9-BBM-718

Just in time

"Just in time," said Stephanie. "There's Patti coming around the park."

"I *knew* she wasn't baby-sitting for Horace," said Kate.

"She's going to be facing this way," I warned.

"Quick — grab a book!" Kate said.

We snatched some books from a pile in the window and held them up in front of our faces, in case Patti's gaze fell on the Bookloft. The three of us lowered our books just far enough so we could peer over them.

Patti locked her bike to the same bench as before. Then she took out a comb and began combing her hair.

"Good grief," Kate said. "Would you look at that!"

"Well, now we know exactly how bad things are," Kate said.

"I'm afraid it's even worse than that," Stephanie said suddenly. "Look at who's following *Patti* around."

Look for these and other books
in the Sleepover Friends Series:

Patti's Secret Wish

Susan Saunders

AN
APPLE
PAPERBACK

SCHOLASTIC INC.
New York Toronto London Auckland Sydney

No part of this publication may be reproduced in whole or in part, or stored in a retrieval system, or transmitted in any form or by any means, electronic, mechanical, photocopying, recording, or otherwise, without written permission of the publisher. For information regarding permission, write to Scholastic Inc., 730 Broadway, New York, NY 10003.

ISBN 0-590-42301-0

Copyright © 1989 by Daniel Weiss Associates, Inc.
All rights reserved. Published by Scholastic Inc. APPLE PAPERBACKS is a registered trademark of Scholastic Inc. SLEEPOVER FRIENDS is a trademark of Scholastic Inc.

12 11 10 9 8 7 6 5 4 3 2 1   9/8 0 1 2 3 4/9

Printed in the U.S.A.   28

First Scholastic printing, June 1989

Chapter 1

"Class, before the final bell rings, I'd like to return the compositions you handed in on Monday," said Mrs. Mead. She pulled a stack of papers out of her desk drawer, stood up, and started passing them out, beginning with the kids in the first row.

Stephanie Green looked at her grade, written in red in the upper right-hand corner of the paper. Then she shrugged her shoulders for Kate Beekman's benefit and mine — I'm Lauren Hunter. Kate and I sit behind Stephanie, in the second row, in Mrs. Mead's fifth-grade class at Riverhurst Elementary.

Kate squinted over Stephanie's shoulder at the grade. "B plus," she murmured.

Maybe there's hope for me, I was thinking, while

Mrs. Mead added her usual, "I would like those of you who received a C plus or lower to rewrite the assignment."

Stephanie and I usually get more or less the same grades, and this time we'd even written on the same topic. Often Mrs. Mead doesn't give the class a choice, but for this assignment there had been two subjects to pick from: We could either imagine we were some kind of insect and write about our adventures, or describe our day as a kitchen appliance.

Based on my years of experience raiding refrigerators, I'd decided to write my composition from the point of view of one — Kate's double-doored refrigerator, in fact. Both of Kate's parents are great cooks, and her fridge is always stuffed with wonderful leftovers. I've put in almost as much time checking out the Beekmans' refrigerator as I have raiding my own.

Stephanie had picked a refrigerator, too. "I certainly couldn't write about bugs," she'd said with a shudder when she and Kate and Patti Jenkins and I were trying to make up our minds last weekend. "Slimy, creepy things, crawling around with all those legs. . . ."

"Bugs really aren't slimy," Patti had pointed out

gently. Patti's great in science. Actually, she's one of the smartest kids in fifth grade, although she never brags about it. "Maybe you're thinking of slugs, or snails, Stephanie — they're . . . um . . . gastropods, I think," she added helpfully.

"Whatever they're called, the only good snail is one in butter sauce," said Stephanie with a sniff, looking at Kate out of the corner of her eye.

"*Yuck!*" Kate gagged. "City people will eat *any-thing*!" She and Stephanie go back and forth so much about what's better, the city or Riverhurst, that it's gotten to be a joke.

It's true that Stephanie is not exactly the outdoor type. She feels more comfortable *indoors*, and she likes to eat as much as I do, even though she's always talking about dieting. "I'll do a refrigerator, too," Stephanie said, "full of fabulous food."

Patti chose ladybugs, because she'd been read-ing about them in a natural history magazine. "They're not just cute little things — even though they *are* your favorite colors," she said, grinning at Stephanie. "They have some pretty interesting habits."

Kate picked insects, too. "A washing machine flips clothes around and around and around, a dish-

3

washer squirts dirty plates with water over and over again, a fridge hums along just keeping the milk cold . . . I'd die of boredom writing a day's worth of that stuff!" Kate hates to be bored. "I think a praying mantis has possibilities: lurking around the garden, snatching up anything that moves and scarfing it down — like Ganthor, in *Ganthor Destroys Manhattan* on last Friday's *Chiller Theater!*"

Kate loves science-fiction movies. In fact, she loves *all* movies: black and white or color, comedy or horror, musicals, silents, old, new. She'd like to be a movie director some day. "I'll write my paper like a science-fiction film!" Kate added excitedly.

Her idea must have worked. When Mrs. Mead gave Kate her composition back, she grinned happily and flashed it at me: A minus!

"Great!" I whispered. I'd turned mine facedown on my desk as soon as Mrs. Mead had handed it to me, trying to work up the nerve to look at it. I'd had some doubts about this one when I turned it in.

"Come on, Lauren," Kate whispered.

"Don't keep us in suspense!" Stephanie hissed over her shoulder.

Slowly, I bent the right-hand corner up . . . Whew!

"B," I reported, vastly relieved. Then I checked out the red marks.

What Mrs. Mead calls "content" wasn't the problem — she'd liked the story. But I would have done better if I hadn't misspelled so many crucial words, like chocolate *mousse* — I knew it wasn't *moose*, or *mouse*, but I thought it might be *mooss*, or *musse* — and veal *scaloppine*. It could just as well have been *scallopene*, couldn't it? Or *scalloppini*? I do have a dictionary, but my room was just a little disorganized that weekend, and I hadn't been able to find it.

Still, I was feeling pretty good about my grade until Karla Stamos leaned forward and murmured in my right ear.

Karla Stamos is one of the biggest grinds at Riverhurst Elementary School. Okay, so she makes good grades — who wouldn't, studying eighteen hours a day? When she's not *in* school, or studying *for* school, she's taking lessons: ballet lessons, violin lessons, poetry lessons, even lessons in how to be a good public speaker.

Karla is kind of a klutz, so maybe the ballet lessons will do her some good. But as far as speaking in public goes, I can't imagine why she'd need lessons. She's never shy about speaking up in class. And she isn't afraid to offer advice, either.

"A *B*, Lauren," Karla whispered as she peered at my paper. "Not bad. But it really does help to use the dictionary, you know. And I'd be happy to lend you my list of commonly misspelled words — it's a handy tool."

Arrgh! I knew she thought she was being really nice, but she made me wish I had another kind of tool handy — like maybe a fly swatter. I could feel my ears getting hot, and they got even hotter when Mrs. Mead handed Karla *her* paper!

Naturally Karla zeroed right in on her own grade, which she was more than happy to share with the rest of us. "A plus!" she said proudly, well above a whisper. "I got an *A plus*!" I guess her public speaking course had told her that repetition helped get your point across.

"Please, nobody ask her what she wrote about," Kate said under her breath, and crossed her fingers. "Or she'll insist on reading us the whole thing."

Mrs. Mead smiled at Karla, but she also put her finger to her lips for Karla to quiet down.

"Yeah, Karla," Mark Freedman grumbled — he sits on Karla's left. "Keep it down. That kind of news gives me an earache." Mark stuck his little finger in his ear and wiggled it around, while Larry Jackson snickered.

Karla ignored them both and started reading her paper — silently, but moving her mouth with a lot of expression, so we'd all know what she was doing and wish we could read the paper, too.

Patti sits in the last desk in the last row. Mrs. Mead got to her just as the bell rang to go home. She handed Patti her paper and raised her voice over the banging of desks and scraping of chairs, "Just a moment, class."

All the kids stopped what they were doing to listen.

"I'd like to see Karla Stamos and Patti Jenkins after school for a few minutes," Mrs. Mead went on.

"Of course, Mrs. Mead," Karla said, beaming like a cat who'd just munched on a four-hundred-pound canary.

"Yes, Mrs. Mead," Patti said, looking surprised.

Stephanie glanced back at Kate and me, and Kate raised a blonde eyebrow.

"All right, class — you're dismissed," said Mrs. Mead.

"Let's get out of here!" I muttered, gathering up

my books and jamming them into my backpack. "I don't think I can take any more of Karla's Helpful Homework Hints today!"

We made signs to Patti that we'd wait for her at the bike rack. Then we rushed out the door of 5B.

"What do you think Mrs. Mead wants?" Stephanie asked as we hurried down the hall.

"Maybe Patti made an A plus, too, and Mrs. Mead wants to post both papers on the bulletin board next to Mrs. Wainwright's office," Kate suggested. Mrs. Wainwright is the principal, and it's a big deal to have your stuff posted on her bulletin board.

"But Patti doesn't make her best grades in writing," Stephanie pointed out.

"It can't be anything serious," I said. "Patti never makes a *bad* grade, and she can't possibly be in any kind of trouble."

"Still . . . ," said Stephanie, frowning thoughtfully.

We walked down the front steps and over to the bike rack.

"Karla's out!" Kate said as we were unlocking our bikes.

Karla was already making her way down the

sidewalk, trying to keep from dropping her pile of books. She latched onto poor Barbara Paulsen from 5C, and from the look on Barbara's face, Karla was either handing out more advice or replaying her "I got an A plus" story.

"I'll ask Karla about Patti," Kate said. She saved Barbara's life at the same time — as soon as Kate walked up to them, Barbara faded into the after-school crowd with a very grateful look on her face.

Kate and Karla talked for a while, until Mrs. Stamos pulled up to the curb in her station wagon and Karla climbed inside.

"What did she say?" Stephanie and I asked Kate when she walked back to the bike rack.

Kate shook her head. "Whatever Mrs. Mead wanted with Patti, she didn't mention it in front of Karla. She told Karla she'd like to print her composition in the *Elementary Review*." That's a school magazine that comes out four times a year. "Karla said her paper was 'all about the adventures of a *beau-ti-ful* butterfly' . . . and then she started to give me the details."

"Ick!" I said.

"Karla is so soppy!" Stephanie groaned.

9

Kate agreed. "Anyway, Mrs. Mead dismissed Karla before she said anything at all to Patti."

So we hadn't really learned anything — except Kate, who knew a little more about the beau-ti-ful butterfly than she wanted to.

Chapter 2

The last school bus loaded up and drove away, down Hillcrest. We could hear some of the guys kicking a soccer ball around on the playground, but the crowds were gone from the front of the school. We were still hanging out at the bike rack.

Kate looked at her watch. "Patti's been in there for almost twenty minutes," she reported.

"Mrs. Mead is cutting into our shopping time at the mall," Stephanie said indignantly. But she tugged at a curl at the back of her head, the way she does when she's worried.

Kate, Stephanie, Patti, and I have been through a lot together. I think each of us feels that if any one of us is having a problem, then we're all having a problem. And a teacher keeping you after school can most definitely fall into the problem area.

The four of us had been planning to bike to the mall after school that day, so there was no way Stephanie and Kate and I would leave without Patti. All for one, and one for all, right? Sometimes it's hard to remember how it was before we were all friends.

Of course, there was a time when there weren't four of us, or even three. In the beginning, it was just Kate and me. We're almost next-door neighbors on Pine Street — there's just one house between us. Kate and I started playing together while we were still in diapers, and by the time we were in kindergarten we were best friends. That's when the sleepovers started — every Friday night, either I'd sleep over at Kate's house, or she'd sleep over at mine. We'd dress up in our moms' clothes and play grownups or school. We'd cook, too. Our idea of cooking in those days was making cherry Kool-Pops in the ice-cube trays, and melting s'mores all over the toaster oven.

Kate's dad, Dr. Beekman, named us the Sleepover Twins, although we couldn't be farther from identical. Kate's small and blonde, I'm tall with darkbrown hair. She's super-neat, I was *born* messy. I love sports, she thinks they're boring. She's always sensible, and I have to admit I've been known to let my imagination run away with me.

Still, they say opposites attract, and for years Kate and I hardly ever had an argument . . . until Stephanie Green moved from the city into a house at the other end of Pine Street, the summer before fourth grade.

Stephanie and I got to know each other because we were both in 4A, Mr. Civello's class. She knew all the latest dance steps, she had her own style of dressing — like mostly wearing red, black, and white, to go with her black hair — and she told great stories about her life back in the city. She was *fun*! I wanted Kate to get to know her, too, so I invited Stephanie to a sleepover at my house.

Major bummer! Kate thought Stephanie was a show-off who only cared about clothes and rock videos. Stephanie thought Kate was bossy and a total know-it-all.

My brother, Roger — he's seventeen — said the problem was obvious. "They're too much alike," he told me. "They're both stubborn and used to getting their own way!"

But I can be plenty stubborn myself, when I have

to be. I didn't give up. Then Stephanie invited Kate and me to spend a Friday night at her house. We stuffed ourselves on Mrs. Green's dynamite peanut-butter-chocolate-chip cookies and watched old movies on Stephanie's private TV, which softened Kate up a little.

The three of us started riding our bikes back and forth to school together and hanging out at the mall or at Charlie's Soda Fountain on weekends. Slowly, Kate and Stephanie began to get used to each other.

Then Patti Jenkins turned up in Mrs. Mead's class this September, along with the three of us. Patti's from the city, too, although you'd never know it to talk to her. She's as quiet and shy as Stephanie is outgoing.

Patti is taller than I am, which is a nice change, since I tower over Kate and Stephanie. She's also a good baseball player, and one of the most thoughtful people I've ever met.

Stephanie wanted Patti to be part of our gang — she and Patti had known each other in kindergarten and first grade back in the city. And Kate and I liked Patti right away. School had barely started, and suddenly there were *four* Sleepover Friends!

"Finally!" Kate said, nodding her head at the front door. "There's Patti."

Patti trudged slowly out of the school building, bouncing her backpack off one knee as she walked.

"Does she look funny to you?" Stephanie murmured to Kate and me.

Patti smiled in our direction, but the smile faded as she headed down the sidewalk to the bike rack.

"It's hard to tell if she's upset or pleased," I said.

"She looks anxious," said Kate.

"Is everything all right?" I asked Patti as soon as she got close enough.

"Of course it is!" Stephanie answered for her. "Mrs. Mead wants to print your composition in the Review, along with Karla's, right?"

"Karla was droning on about it while you were still inside," Kate explained.

"Karla is such a show-off, always letting everyone know how good her grades are . . . ," said Stephanie.

"They ought to be! She doesn't have a life outside of school and studying!" I added, still hearing Karla's voice in my ear.

Patti just stood there with that strange expression

on her face, so Kate went on. "I mean, she wants to be nice, but if she keeps this up, nobody will even talk to her."

"And why does she always wear brown?" Stephanie filled in, since Patti wasn't talking. "It's such a boring color. Who looks good in brown, except maybe Mrs. Norris's poodle." Mrs. Norris lives at the front end of Pine Street, and her poodle, Max, has a brown turtleneck sweater.

Stephanie, Kate, and I giggled, but all Patti could manage was a small grin.

"So . . . is that it? Your paper'll be in the Review?" I asked.

"Uh . . . no . . . Mrs. Mead did talk to me about my paper," Patti said, looking down at her feet. "She . . . um . . . told me to do it over," she added finally.

So that was what the strange expression meant — Patti was really embarrassed!

"Do it over!" Stephanie exclaimed. "You couldn't have made a C plus or lower!"

I don't think Patti's ever gotten lower than an A minus in her life, although she'd never say so.

"Uh . . . it wasn't that, exactly," Patti replied. "My information was okay, it just wasn't very . . . very . . ."

16

"Creative?" Stephanie guessed.

"Right!" Patti agreed quickly. "It wasn't creative enough."

"No problem," said Kate. "Four imaginations are better than one, especially if one of them is outrageous. . . ." She poked me with her toe and grinned.

"Thanks, Kate," I said, making a face at her.

"In other words, we'll help you, Patti," said Kate. "Let's see your paper."

"Oh!" Patti sort of jumped, and fumbled with the zipper on her backpack. "I . . . I don't have it. Mrs. Mead kept it."

"That doesn't matter, we know what it's about: ladybugs," said Kate.

"You could start it with the nursery rhyme," suggested Stephanie. "You know: 'Ladybug, ladybug, fly away home. . . .' "

"That's not a bad idea," Kate said. "And then maybe describe the ladybug's home. . . ."

"And her children," I said, still thinking of the nursery rhyme. "Are they eggs, or worms, or what?"

"Lauren — please!" Stephanie said, clutching her stomach.

17

"We'll work on it at my house tomorrow night," Kate told Patti. It was Kate's turn that week to have the Friday-night sleepover.

"Now that that's settled, we can go to the mall," said Stephanie, pulling her bike out of the rack.

"Um . . . I have to . . . I can't go with you," Patti said hurriedly.

"Why not?" Kate asked, puzzled. We'd all planned this trip several days before.

Patti ducked her head. "I . . . uh . . . Mrs. Mead wants my composition back first thing tomorrow," she replied. "I'd better go home and get started on it."

Stephanie shrugged her shoulders. "Okay, then we won't go to the mall, either. We'll go home with you. . . ."

"And help you with your paper," I finished.

"Right," said Kate. "We can go to the mall on Saturday."

"Oh," said Patti, swallowing hard. "Thanks, guys, but I think I'd better work on my paper alone. You've already given me some great ideas," she added quickly, "but I'd feel really bad if you gave up the trip to the mall."

"Are you sure?" said Stephanie.

"I'm sure," Patti said. Her cheeks were turning pink.

"All right," Stephanie said.

The four of us got on our bikes and started up Hillcrest. Nobody said much until we were almost at the corner of Pine Street. Then Stephanie said to Kate and me, "Would you mind stopping at my house first? I've got a sweater I want to exchange at Just Juniors."

"Okay," Kate and I agreed.

We all braked our bikes and coasted over to the sidewalk.

"Well, I guess I'll be heading on home," Patti said. She lives on Mill Road, which is farther up Hillcrest. "Have a good time."

"Good luck with your paper," said Kate.

"Bye," said Patti, pedaling away.

"See you tomorrow morning," Stephanie and I called out.

We watched Patti until she'd disappeared over the top of the hill. Then the three of us looked at each other.

Kate raised an eyebrow. "What was that all about? Patti was acting sort of strange, don't you think?"

19

"She didn't want us with her, that's for sure," Stephanie said.

"She's just embarrassed about her composition," I said. "She's not used to having problems with her schoolwork. It takes some practice — I should know."

Kate and Stephanie grinned.

"You're probably right," said Stephanie. "Anyway, let's get going!" We pedaled around the corner and whizzed down Pine Street toward the Greens' house. "If we hurry," she added, "we can squeeze in a slice at the Pizza Palace before dinner!"

Chapter
3

Before we could *see* Stephanie's house, we could *hear* it.

"What's that awful noise?" Kate said as we glided around the curve on Pine Street. "It sounds like a gigantic washing machine that's falling apart!"

"The cement truck," Stephanie replied with a sigh. "First it was the bulldozer, then the backhoe, and now it's the cement truck."

The Greens were adding a wing onto their house, which meant that a lot of trees had to be knocked down, a hole dug for the foundation, and then the foundation poured. The cement truck was parked in their front yard. The huge mixer was white with big blue and pink polka-dots. It was pouring

21

thick, wet concrete down a long chute into an enormous hole at one end of the lawn.

"Watch out for the rocks and dirt," Stephanie warned as we turned into the driveway. "Who ever would have thought that one baby could make such a mess?" she added.

All of her life, Stephanie has been the only child in the Green family. But now her mom is expecting a baby. Stephanie claims she's really looking forward to having a little sister or brother, but Kate and Patti and I all come from two-kid families, and we have our doubts.

As Kate puts it, "Stephanie's used to being the big cheese. She's got her own telephone, her own TV, her own VCR — what if she has to share them? How is she going to like it when she isn't the center of attention anymore?"

We leaned our bikes against the Greens' garage and were headed into the kitchen when Kate said, "Another foundation?"

Toward the back fence, about thirty feet from the house, there was a smallish, rectangular hole cut into the grass.

"Your dad's having a pool put in!" I said, always hopeful.

Stephanie shook her head. "Nope — we'll just have to keep swimming at the Health Club on Main. It's going to be an office for my dad," she told us. Mr. Green's a lawyer, and he does a lot of work on weekends.

Stephanie pushed open the kitchen door and called out, "Hi, Mom! It's us!"

"Hi, girls — I'm in here!" Mrs. Green was lying on a bunch of pillows on the living room floor, and she was huffing and puffing like the Little Engine That Could!

Stephanie's kitten, Cinders, didn't seem worried — he was sound asleep on the couch. But Kate asked anxiously, "Are you okay?"

Mrs. Green laughed and sat up. "I'm fine," she said. "Just practicing my breathing exercises. I thought you girls were going to the mall after school today."

"We are, but I decided to return that sweater I bought last Sunday at Just Juniors — it's too much like the one Nana sent me from the city," Stephanie said.

"Where's Patti?" Mrs. Green asked as we headed down the hall to Stephanie's room.

"She went home," Stephanie answered over her

23

shoulder. "She had homework to do."

Stephanie closed the door to her bedroom, and Kate and I flopped down on her red-black-and white-striped twin beds. Stephanie's whole room is done in her favorite colors. The two foam-rubber chairs that unfold into spare beds are covered in red denim, there's a black-and-white rug on the floor, her phone is red, her floor lamp is white, and even her *kitten* goes with the color scheme: Cinders is solid black.

"You know what's weird?" Stephanie said to us, lowering her voice.

"What?" Kate and I answered.

"My birthday's in ten days, right?" Stephanie opened her closet door.

"Right," Kate and I said. She and Patti and I had already pooled our funds to buy Stephanie's present — a great-looking, red-and-black corduroy jumper from Dandelion, a kids' store on Main Street. It was wrapped up at Patti's house.

"My parents haven't even mentioned it!" Stephanie said gloomily. She pulled out a shopping bag from Just Juniors and frowned at herself in the mirror on the inside of the closet door. "They haven't said a single word about a party, or even a present."

"Really?" Kate said, sounding very solemn. She

24

and I didn't look at each other on purpose, because we were afraid we'd start giggling.

We didn't know anything about a present from the Greens, but Stephanie's dad had talked to Kate and Patti and me days before about the party. He was going to rent the whole Pizza Palace — okay, it's not exactly as big as a palace, but still — from two to five in the afternoon a week from the coming Saturday. John the cook would be there, baking as many pizzas as everybody could eat in three hours, plus there would be unlimited sodas and free video games and songs on the jukebox! Mr. Green had asked us for a list of twenty names of the kids we thought Stephanie might like to have come.

The girls were pretty easy: Stephanie and the three of us, of course, Jane Sykes, Sally Mason, Nancy Hersh, Erin Wilson, and Robin Becker from Mrs. Mead's class, and Tracy Osner from 5A. Patti, Kate, and I had talked about Karla Stamos, too, but that would have made eleven girls — and she was just *too* boring.

The boys were a lot harder, because we change our minds about them a lot more often. Mark Freedman and Larry Jackson from 5B, of course — we don't have any problems with them. Probably Todd

Farrell from 5A — he's Jane Sykes' cousin. He's really nice, and Patti likes him, sort of. Michael Pastore from 5A — Stephanie used to like him, but now they're just friends; Kyle Hubbard, also from 5A — he's good friends with Kate because they were in the same fourth-grade class and because they're both science-fiction movie freaks; Henry Larkin, in our class this year, who's gone from being a geek to being really cute; and Alan Reese, from 5A, who's always fun. But then there's David Degan from our class, who's turning into macho man; Pete Stone, who can't seem to make up his mind if he likes Jenny Carlin — the boy-craziest girl in fifth grade — or me, not that I care. And Stephanie's always talking about how cute Donald Foster is — he lives in the house between Kate's and mine, he's in the seventh grade, and he's the most conceited boy in Riverhurst. Would Stephanie want him to come to her party?

"Really," Stephanie was saying. "They're so into this baby thing, it's like nothing else exists! I honestly think they haven't planned anything." She closed her closet door with a bang. "Ready?"

"Have you hinted?" I asked. Stephanie's a great hinter when she wants something.

Stephanie nodded. "Nothing seems to work," she said. "Just watch."

We walked back into the living room, where Mrs. Green was huffing and puffing again. "We're going, Mom," Stephanie said. "Maybe I'll see something I really like . . . something special. . . ."

"Have fun, girls," said Mrs. Green. "Huff . . . huff . . . huff. . . ." She blew all of her breath out in one great "whoooosh!"

Stephanie rolled her eyes at Kate and me and waved good-bye to her mother.

Outside, she hooked the shopping bag over one of her handlebars. "If we push our bikes down the Williamses' alley" — the Williamses live in the house behind the Greens' — "and cut through the vacant lot over to Bellows Lane and then to Halsey, we'll get to the mall a lot faster," Stephanie suggested.

"Sounds good," said Kate.

"The faster we get there, the better," I said. "I'm starving!"

We ended up riding across the University campus, because Halsey Road runs right through it. The campus is a bunch of old stone buildings and a handful of tall, modern buildings, all grouped around Griffen Park. The park is long and narrow, with maple trees growing along the edges, a dolphin fountain splashing away in the middle, and usually a lot of college hunks hanging out on the grass.

We slowed down to watch two guys flying a kite, and a spotted dog retrieving a Frisbee, when Stephanie suddenly screeched to a stop. "Hey, look — isn't that Patti's bike?" She pointed to a navy-blue bike locked to a bench in front of one of the older buildings.

Kate and I braked next to Stephanie. "It can't be," Kate said. "Patti was going straight home."

"Oh, yeah?" Stephanie said. "How many navy-blue Rosses are tooling around Riverhurst with the initials PLJ stenciled on their frames in gold?" The L is for Lucia.

Kate and I leaned closer to check out the small gold letters. "Not many," we agreed. It had to be Patti's.

"She's probably visiting her parents," Kate said then.

Patti's parents are both history professors at the University. Mrs. Jenkins teaches ancient history, and Mr. Jenkins modern.

I shook my head. "Not here," I said. I pointed to the name of the building, carved into the reddish stone above the door. "Lindeman is the science building. I came here once with my dad, to take a science professor to look at a house." My father sells real estate for Blaney Realty. "The history building is all the way across the park — Hodges, I think it's called."

"So what's Patti doing at Lindeman, when she's supposed to be fixing up her composition, instead of going to the mall with us?" said Stephanie, frowning at the front of the building.

"Ssst!" Kate hissed. "Come on, let's get behind the maple!"

"But it's Patti!" Stephanie said, starting forward.

"She's not alone!" Kate grabbed Stephanie's arm, and pulled her behind the tree with us.

Patti was standing just inside the wide front doors of Lindeman, and she was talking to one of the best-looking guys I'd ever seen, outside of TV or the movies.

He was probably in his early twenties, with straight, reddish-brown hair combed to one side, dark eyes, and a light tan. He was wearing a bright-green cable sweater, old khakis, and white sneakers.

And he was smiling down at Patti, who was beaming up at him.

As we watched from behind the maple, he pointed farther into the building with his right hand. He put his left hand on Patti's backpack and kind of moved her along, out of sight.

"Well?" I said.

"Well . . ." Kate said.

"Well!" said Stephanie.

What else could we say?

Chapter
4

"He's probably a friend of Patti's parents," Stephanie said firmly. "Or a student who's been to their house. John, could I have another slice, with pepperoni and extra cheese?" By then we were sitting at the counter at the Pizza Palace in the mall. All the thinking we'd been doing had made us very hungry. Stephanie added dreamily, "Doesn't he look a little like Kevin DeSpain?"

Kevin DeSpain is our favorite actor. He's one of the stars on "Made for Each Other," which is on TV every Tuesday night at eight-thirty. Kevin has dark hair and big green eyes. "Would Patti's guy be better looking with green eyes?" Stephanie asked.

I thought back to the dark hair and dark eyes

and the tan. . . . "How *could* he be?" I said.

"If he's a friend of the Jenkinses, then why haven't we heard about him before?" Kate asked, sticking to the point as usual. "We tell each other everything." She was finishing her second Dr Pepper and a slice of meatball pizza.

"He was *not* somebody Patti bumped into and asked for directions — she definitely knew him," I said. "John, I'd like another Dr Pepper and another slice of Sicilian style — thanks. And she *hasn't* told us about him. So. . . ," I went on, "the only logical explanation is — Patti's leading a *double life*!" The idea was so exciting that I drank most of Kate's DP by mistake. "Remember that movie we saw two Fridays ago on TV? It was called *His Double Life* and the guy had a second family that no one else knew about. . . ."

Stephanie and Kate tapped their heads and grinned at each other.

"She's off and running," said Stephanie.

"*Lau-ren,*" said Kate, in the tone she uses when she thinks my imagination has gone out of control. "*Logical?*"

"Of course! Patti's adopted, and that's her long-lost older brother from a family that doesn't include

32

Mr. and Mrs. Jenkins and little brother Horace,"
Stephanie said. Then she and Kate snickered into
their napkins.

"I think it sounds very romantic," I said stiffly.
The other two burst into giggles.

"As far as I can see, there are only two reasons
why Patti wouldn't have told us about him," Stephanie said, pulling herself together. "Either she never
laid eyes on him until this afternoon, which doesn't
seem very likely" — Stephanie took her fresh slice
from John and folded it lengthwise — "Or . . .
um . . ." — she took a big bite, and sucked in a long
string of melted cheese into her mouth — "or she's
embarrassed. Like she was about her composition,
which she didn't want to tell us about, either, remember?"

"Embarrassed about what?" Kate said, not following.

"Embarrassed about having a crush on a college
guy, of course!" Stephanie said. "Maybe she met
him recently, like at the party at the University Club
that she went to last Thursday with her parents. But
it doesn't really matter where or when. The fact is,
a crush would explain why she rushed off to hang
around Lindeman where she knew he'd be, and it

would also explain why she didn't do very well on her composition. She *couldn't concentrate!*"

"Patti with a crush. . . ," Kate said.

Patti seemed too sensible to have a crush on a *much* older guy. Besides, it was hard for me to imagine Patti liking any guy so much that she'd let it mess up her homework.

"There's an easy way to find out," said Kate. "We'll *ask* her."

"We can't do that!" Stephanie said. "She'll think we've been spying on her!"

"So what do we do?" I asked. "Forget we ever saw him?"

"Get real!" said Stephanie. "We give her two minutes to tell us herself . . . and then we hint like crazy!"

"Yo! Girls!" Mark Freedman barreled through the door of the Pizza Palace just about then, with Larry Jackson right behind him.

"Yo, Mark," we said.

"Dibs on Alien Attackers!" Larry shouted, shoving Mark out of the way with a body block and dropping a quarter into his favorite video game before Mark could recover.

34

Mark shrugged coolly and grabbed Turkey Shoot.

Electrified buzzes and squeaks and squawks filled the room as Mark and Larry pushed buttons and wiggled handles. Then there was an incredibly loud, totally rude noise that made Stephanie, Kate, and me spin around on our stools.

David Degan was standing just inside the door with one hand under his arm and a satisfied smirk on his freckled face. "I do it with my armpit," he said to Larry and Mark, who had actually stopped fiddling with the video games for a second.

"Can you believe I used to think he was cute? Gross me out!" Stephanie muttered. "Let's go to Just Juniors — no boys!"

Kate and I glanced at each other, and she made a thumbs-down sign. David Degan was definitely off the birthday list.

Our first opportunity to pump Patti was on the way to school the next morning. Stephanie, Kate, and I met her at the corner of Pine Street at eight-thirty, the way we always do.

As soon as the four of us were pedaling down

Hillcrest toward Riverhurst Elementary, Kate said, "Did you redo your composition yesterday afternoon, Patti?"

"Oh . . . yes," Patti said, without taking her eyes off the road.

"That's good," said Kate.

Stephanie waited a second and said, "We went to the mall a new way yesterday."

"Oh, really?" Patti said. "How?"

"We cut down the Williamses' alley — " Stephanie began, but Patti interrupted her.

"You did? Did you see Walter?" she asked, giving Stephanie a worried look.

Walter Williams is a seven-and-a-half-year-old genius with reddish hair, a skinny neck, and ears that stick out. He has an IQ of 175 or 190 or something incredible like that, and instead of being in the second or third grade where he belongs, he's already a fourth-grader.

"No — Walter was probably squirreled away inside the house, playing with his computers," Kate said. "Why do you ask?" she added, squinting at Patti. Kate's supposed to wear glasses, but she hardly ever does.

"Oh . . . no reason," Patti said, looking back

36

at the road while her face turned pink. "Which way did you go after the Williamses' alley?"

"Through the vacant lot, over to Bellows Lane, and then all the way up Halsey," I said.

Patti jerked the front wheel of her bike and almost went over. We were making her so jumpy that I felt bad for her.

I guess Kate and Stephanie did, too, because they changed the subject. "There was a big shipment of new clothes in at Just Juniors," Stephanie said.

"Yeah — we saw a blue-and-yellow plaid sweater with matching denim pegged pants that would look terrific on you, Patti," Kate told her. "Hey — Dad's working at the hospital tonight. If you guys could come over early, Mom might drive us to the mall. We could spend some more time trying on stuff and then have dinner at the Burger Joint!"

"Great!" Stephanie and I exclaimed at the same time.

But Patti looked horrified. "I . . . I can't! I have to . . . to stay with Horace until seven, because . . . because Mom and Dad'll be at a conference at the University until then. . . ."

We'd reached Riverhurst Elementary, so we got off our bikes and walked them over to the rack.

Patti looked upset enough to cry. "I'm really sorry," she said, her lip sort of trembling.

"That's okay," Kate said cheerfully. "Forget about the Burger Joint — we'll have Chinese take-out waiting when you get to my house at seven."

I mean, we weren't trying to drive Patti *crazy* — we just wanted to figure out what was going on!

Chapter
5

"What was that business about Walter Williams?" Stephanie whispered to me. The first bell had rung, and we were following Kate and Patti into the school building.

"Beats me," I whispered back.

She started to snicker. "Maybe he's part . . . part of P-Patti's double life, too," Stephanie said. She was giggling so much she could barely get the words out. "You know — Patti's *other*, long-lost *younger* brother. S-sorry," Stephanie added when I frowned at her.

After the second bell had rung and class was about to start, Kate wrote something on a scrap of paper and slid it onto my desk: "Bet you a dollar that Patti's going back to Lindeman after school today."

As soon as I'd read it, Kate pointed at Stephanie's back, so I stuck the note into Stephanie's belt.

She looked at the note, nodded, and scribbled something herself on the bottom. When I unfolded the paper wad she dropped at my feet, I read, "SO WILL *WE!*"

During class that morning, Patti didn't hand in the composition she was supposed to have rewritten. Mrs. Mead never asked for it, either. Had Patti made the whole thing up? Why would she?

In the cafeteria at noon, she still seemed jumpy, even though Kate and Stephanie and I didn't go anywhere near the subject we were most interested in: *Who was that amazing guy we say you with yesterday?* We came up with something else to focus on at lunch: Pete Stone and Jenny Carlin.

Jenny Carlin's in Mrs. Mead's class, too. She's small, with tiny hands and feet, this button nose that tilts up just a little, and long, dark hair. As far as I can tell, she spends every waking second thinking about boys, and probably every sleeping second, too. I think all the girls in Riverhurst could drop off the face of the earth, and Jenny Carlin wouldn't no-

40

tice they were gone. Actually, she *might* notice if her sidekick, Angela Kemp, disappeared, but only because Jenny would miss the sound of all those "yesses" Angela gives her.

Anyway, I don't like Jenny Carlin, and Jenny Carlin can't stand me. At the beginning of the year, she decided that the boy she liked most was Pete Stone. Then, for some reason, Pete Stone started liking me!

It made Jenny furious, and she went around telling anybody who would listen that I was chasing after Pete! Chasing after him?! Give me a break! Although he is kind of cute.

As it turns out, Pete is almost as flakey as Jenny. One week he's hanging on her every word, and the next week he's trying to go jogging with me — I jog every other day with Roger, my brother.

Obviously, this was Jenny Carlin week, because Pete Stone was sitting at her table in the cafeteria with a silly grin on his face, watching her bat her eyelashes.

"Oh, Pete!" Jenny screeched. "You're *so* funny!"

I sighed and made a thumbs-down sign to Kate. I didn't know how Stephanie felt about Pete Stone at that moment, but *I* certainly didn't want him at the birthday party. So we'd already lost two from the boys' list.

Then Mark and Larry and Henry Larkin flopped down at our table, and Stephanie said, "Henry, why do you have that frankfurter stuck in your ear?" — lunch was franks and beans that day — and Henry said, "What? I can't hear you. There's a frankfurter stuck in my ear." Which was goofy, but it was *okay* goofy. All of us like Henry. Maybe we could add Bobby Krieger from 5C and Tommy Brown . . . or was Kate still mad at Bobby for liking Christy Soames? I'd have to ask her.

Anyway, with the boys scarfing down our leftovers and kidding around, we couldn't have talked to Patti about Lindeman if we'd wanted to. And the minute school was over that afternoon, she rushed off!

"I have to leave you guys and race home," she apologized as we started down the front walk at school. "Mom doesn't like Horace to be alone, even for a minute, and his bus has already left. See you tonight!" And she trotted away.

"Right!" The three of us waved and smiled.

But as soon as Patti was pedaling safely up Hillcrest, Stephanie barked, "Let's *hit it*! To Pine Street and then the back way to Halsey. It's a cinch, we'll get to the University before she does."

Since I have longer legs than Stephanie and Kate, I took the lead — I actually had to slow down a little so that I wouldn't run over Patti from behind. I raced around the corner of Pine, coasted past the curve, and zoomed up Stephanie's driveway.

A big truck from A-1 Lumber Company was parked next to the garage, and two men in overalls were unloading large sheets of plywood.

"The walls," Stephanie explained when she and Kate caught up with me.

We pushed our bikes between the truck and the garage, past the little foundation for Mr. Green's office, and down the Williamses' alley. This time we looked around for Walter, mainly because Patti had acted so odd about him.

But the Williamses' yard was empty, except for Bob, Walter's dog. "If you want to see something odd, check out that mutt," Stephanie said — Bob's half Dalmatian and half Bassett Hound, and he was sprawled across the back steps like a mildewy pillow.

"He looks exactly like the spotted caterpillars

that ate my mom's tomato plants," Kate giggled.

Out of the alley, we bumped across the vacant lot next to the Bluebird Nursery School and over to Bellows Lane. Then we zoomed up Halsey to the campus without slowing down.

"Don't park near Lindeman," Kate warned. "Patti'll see our bikes, just like we saw hers."

We needed to find a good place for a stake-out. . . . "What about the Bookloft?" I suggested. The Bookloft is the University bookstore, two buildings over from Lindeman, with a plate-glass window that sticks way out onto the sidewalk. "From inside the window, we'd have a clear view of the Lindeman front steps," I pointed out.

"And there are lots of bikes out front — safety in numbers," said Stephanie approvingly. It's kind of hard to disguise a custom-painted, red-black-and-white-checked fifteen speed.

We pushed our bikes into the crowd at the rack in front of the Bookloft and locked them up. Then we dashed up the steps.

"You'll have to check your backpacks," said a guard just inside the door.

"Okay, but hurry!" Stephanie squealed, standing on her tiptoes to try to see over the shoppers and out the window.

The guard took our packs and gave us each a plastic number. Then we pushed through a turnstile and into the store.

"Can I help you find what you're looking for?" asked a cute guy wearing a plaid shirt and a blue jacket with "Bookloft" on the pocket.

"No, thank you. We're just looking for the window," Kate said hurriedly. We dodged around some tables and bookcases and took up our positions just behind the plate glass.

"This may take a while," Stephanie said.

But we hadn't been standing there long when who should appear but the Mystery Man!

He was walking slowly up the sidewalk toward Lindeman, wearing a navy-blue sweater, a pink shirt, gray pleated pants, and brown moccasins.

"I think he looks even better than yesterday," Kate said. The three of us were absolutely *gawking* out the window at him.

"He's gorgeous," Stephanie murmured. "I mean, I can understand why Patti — "

We all poked each other with elbows at the same

45

time. A tall, lanky girl with blonde hair was chasing the Mystery Man down the sidewalk!

"Jeff," she yelled, so loudly we could hear her through the plate glass.

"He has a name," murmured Kate.

Jeff whirled around, held his arms out, and the girl ran right into them.

"Just like an ad on TV," Stephanie said.

"For shampoo," I added, because the girl really had beautiful hair — thick, blonde, wavy, everything that mine isn't.

"She's stunning," said Stephanie, and I guess she was, in a bony sort of way. She was wearing a long, dark-purple paisley dress, tights, and ankle boots. "She looks like a model," Stephanie added. Stephanie knew some models when she lived in the city.

Jeff and the model hugged for a while. Then they gave each other a big kiss, right in the middle of the sidewalk! Nobody paid any attention to them, except us — I guess middle-of-the-afternoon sidewalk kissing isn't unusual at universities.

"Oooh, poor Patti!" Stephanie groaned.

"I hope she doesn't see this," Kate said, leaning

even farther into the window to peer up and down the street for Patti.

"I think they're about to break it up. . . ," I said.

"Hurry, hurry," Stephanie muttered, concentrating hard on the two kissers.

Jeff and the model finally pulled their lips apart. They backed a step away from each other, and just held hands for a second or two while they talked. We couldn't hear what they were saying, of course, but it seemed very friendly.

They kissed one more time. Then Jeff ran up the steps of Lindeman, and the model walked back the way she came, looking very happy.

"Just in time," said Stephanie. "There's Patti, coming around the park."

"I *knew* she wasn't baby-sitting for Horace," said Kate.

"She's going to be facing this way," I warned.

"Quick — grab a book!" Kate said.

We snatched some books from a pile in the window and held them up in front of our faces, in case Patti's gaze fell on the Bookloft.

"She's undoubtedly looking for *him*!" Stephanie said. The three of us had lowered our books just far

47

enough so we could peer over them.

Patti locked her bike to the same bench as before. Then she took out a small mirror and a comb and began combing her hair.

"Good grief," Kate said. "Would you look at that!"

"Well, now we know exactly how bad things are," Kate said. "Patti has a crush on a college guy — "

". . . who has a knock-out girlfriend," I went on.

"I'm afraid it's even worse than that," Stephanie said suddenly. "Look at who's following *Patti* around."

"Walter Williams!" Kate and I both exclaimed.

Walter was tearing down the sidewalk in his old orange down vest, his reddish hair poking up like straw, his ears sticking out. His brown glasses bounced up and down on his nose as he raced up the steps after Patti.

"Remember what a pest he was when he had a crush on you, Lauren?" Stephanie said.

"Don't remind me!" Walter Williams had decided he was in love with me the first time we met, and it got very embarrassing for a while. I mean, Walter's only seven and a half years old. . . .

"Wow — do you think that's how Jeff feels about Patti?" I wondered out loud. I was only *three* years older than Walter, and Jeff was probably *ten* years older than Patti, at least. What must he be thinking?

"Aaaa-hmmm!" It was the cute salesclerk in the blue jacket clearing his throat at us. "Would you ladies like to buy those books, or do you just want to hold them?"

"Well . . . uh . . ." We glanced down at the books we'd been clutching in front of our faces: *Lasers, Quasars, and Quarks*.

"We'll just hold them, thank you," said Kate.

Chapter
6

Around six o'clock that night, Stephanie and I went with Mrs. Beekman, Kate, and Kate's little sister, Melissa the Monster, to get Chinese take-out. Ben Luck's is all the way around the loop, near Tully's Fish Market, so we didn't really expect to run into anybody we knew. But we'd barely gotten to the bottom of Column A on the menu when Donald Foster walked into the restaurant with his dad.

"Hey, ladies," Donald drawled, flashing his best movie-star smile. "What's happening?"

I guess he expected us to drop dead over his blond good looks, or something, but Kate and I both said, "Yuck!" under our breath.

Besides thinking he's the most wonderful thing that ever happened to women, Donald teases us a lot. Since he lives in the house between Kate's and mine, he's seen plenty of sleepover messes that we'd just as soon forget — like the time the water main broke on Pine Street, and we couldn't wash the purple styling gel out of our hair; or the time he spotted us sneaking across the backyard with green avocado masks on our faces; or the time he saw us taking a trip with a donkey. . . . I could go on for hours. Donald has never forgotten a single episode, and he loves to remind us of them at choice moments, like in front of six or eight boys at Charlie's Soda Fountain.

In spite of all that, Stephanie is always saying how great-looking she thinks he is. I guess Melissa agrees with her. Melissa's only in the second grade, and she's a real pain — always trying to get in on whatever Kate's doing. But this was something new. She batted her eyelashes like a smaller version of Jenny Carlin, and squealed, "Hi-i-i-i, Donald!"

When he said, "Hi, Squirt," I thought she was going to swoon!

"He is so-o-o cute!" Stephanie said as Donald sat down at a table with his father. "He's looking more and more like Carter Grant, don't you think?'' Carter Grant is one of the stars of *Surftown*, on Mondays.

''More like Gumby,'' muttered Kate. ''Should we get spring rolls or egg rolls?'' She pointed to Column B of the take-out menu.

But with her other hand she made a thumbs-up sign to me. We'd definitely have to put Donald down on the birthday list, whether *we* wanted him or not. Maybe we'd get lucky — maybe he'd decide that an important seventh-grader couldn't possibly go to a lowly fifth-grade party.

It's always a mistake to get take-out when you're really hungry: you're afraid that you'll end up back home with too little food, so you order enough for ten people. That's what happened that night, anyway. We had spring rolls *and* egg rolls, spare ribs in black bean sauce, sweet-and-sour shrimp, pork-fried rice, steamed dumplings, and even *I* can't remember what else.

Melissa drives us crazy if we eat in the kitchen, so Mrs. Beekman said we could take our containers up to Kate's room. We had to make several trips with all the Chinese food, plus two giant-size Dr Peppers, glasses, ice, plates, and a platter of Kate's super-fudge. We stacked everything on Kate's desk and dresser to keep it out of the way of Fredericka, Kate's kitten, who was prowling around on the floor. Then we lugged the Beekmans' old portable TV into her bedroom — we always borrow it for our sleep-overs — and closed the door in Melissa's nosy face.

"I hope Patti comes soon," Stephanie said, opening one of the cartons and poking a finger in the sauce. "I'm starving — it was all that racing around this afternoon."

"Yeah, me, too," I said, breaking off a tiny corner of super-fudge.

"You're always hungry, Lauren," Kate said, slapping my hand. "Before Patti gets here, we have to decide: Are we going to clue her in about Jeff's girlfriend? She really should know."

"I still think we have to let her tell *us* about Jeff first," Stephanie said, lifting the flaps of another carton and eyeing the dumplings hungrily.

"We already tried that," I pointed out. "It didn't work."

"Ah, yes," said Stephanie, "but tonight we have the secret weapon."

"What secret weapon?" Kate asked.

"Truth or Dare!" Stephanie snagged a shrimp and popped it into her mouth.

Bang. Melissa hit the other side of Kate's door so hard that Fredericka raced under the bed and Stephanie almost choked on her shrimp.

"Go away!" Kate shouted.

"Patti's here!" Melissa shrieked back.

Patti was already up the stairs when Kate opened the door to tell Melissa to leave us alone. Patti didn't *look* funny, like she had that morning when she'd mentioned Walter Williams and the new route we'd taken to the mall. She looked like her old self, and she gave us a big grin. But she sure *smelled* funny.

I have a terrific nose. I can sniff out a new bakery from several blocks away, tell the difference between most of my mom's herbs and spices without looking at the labels, and find my sneakers in the dark. The minute Patti walked into Kate's bedroom that night, I couldn't help but notice that she smelled like Kate's dad after he's been at the hospital: a combination of rubbing alcohol and green soap and whatever else doctors use. Is it some kind of perfume? I wondered. Because if it is, it ought to be called "Afternoon at the Hospital."

I glanced over at Kate and Stephanie, but they hadn't picked up on it. Kate has allergies and was sort of sniffy that evening, and Stephanie's nose was still too close to the shrimp.

"Okay — who wants what?" Kate asked, opening the rest of the Chinese-food cartons.

"I want a little of everything," Stephanie said. "After all the work I did this aft — " She stopped short — she'd almost given us away!

"What did you guys do this afternoon?" Patti asked, taking a spring roll and some pork-fried rice.

"Oh, we hung out at Stephanie's house — did some exercises Roger taught me," I said quickly.

"My parents still haven't said a word about my birthday," Stephanie told Patti. "No party and nothing about a present. I've hinted and hinted, but I'm about to give up on them."

"We'll have a party at the sleepover next Friday," Patti said — it would be Stephanie's turn. "Just the four of us."

"Yeah — Lauren and you and I can make a cake that afternoon, Patti," Kate said.

"Right," Patti said with a smile. Then she got that funny expression on her face again. "Oh — I'm busy on Friday afternoon. I . . . uh . . . have an appointment with . . . uh . . . Dr. Nadler." Dr. Nadler's the dentist we all go to.

"What about Thursday, then?" I suggested. "The cake would stay fresh overnight in the refrigerator."

"N-no, Thursday's no good, either." Patti put down her fork and looked very uncomfortable. "I . . . uh . . . I have to. . . . Maybe we could do it Wednesday!"

"A two-day-old cake?" Kate said doubtfully.

"Hey, listen — that's okay." Stephanie said, shrugging her shoulders. "I'll ask Mom to buy an ice-cream cake at Russell's for the sleepover. No big deal."

But I could tell her feelings were hurt. Stephanie didn't have a clue about the party at the Pizza Palace. She really thought her parents were too involved with baby stuff. And now she was probably thinking Patti would rather lurk around the University, hoping to run into Jeff, than help bake a birthday cake.

Maybe Melissa the Monster wasn't the only one turning into another version of Jenny Carlin, boy-chaser. Would it get to the point where Stephanie and Kate and I could drop off the face of the earth, and Patti wouldn't even notice?

"Anybody want seconds?" Kate said brightly into the silence.

We managed to find room for some more Chinese food. After we'd fed the pork strips in the leftover fried rice to Fredericka, we got down to work on Kate's super-fudge and turned on her radio to listen to WBRM.

WBRM is a Riverhurst station, and on Friday and Saturday nights Rockin' Ralphie plays requests. Most of them are from Riverhurst High students, although sometimes there is a dedication from somebody in junior high. Once in a while we even hear an elementary-school request. As a matter of fact, a few months ago, we phoned in a joke request for Jenny Carlin ourselves.

It's fun to try to figure out who is who. Usually it's easy like, Todd S. and Mary Beth Y. Todd Schwartz is quarterback of the high-school football team — he lives across the street from Stephanie. Mary Beth Young is his steady girlfriend, more or less. They break up practically weekly. By paying attention to whether the request is something like, "Always, Forever," by the Jayvees or "Tired of Your Ways," by Oxo, you can keep track of their romance on WBRM.

Tugg K. is Tugg Keeler, a Riverhurst High tackle. Barbara B. is Barbara Baxter, his girlfriend who's a cheerleader, and they're always on WBRM. We even heard a dedication to my brother once. We never figured out who the girl was, because she only gave her initials, D. L. — Doreen Lucas? Debbie Lawrence? DeeDee Lorch? — but we teased Roger about it for weeks!

"This next request is from Becky M. to Tony J. 'Too Soon to Tell,' by Pard!" Rockin' Ralphie shouted. "Hang in there, Tony!"

"Who's Becky M.?" Stephanie asked, rolling over on the floor to snag another piece of fudge. "Am *I* stuffed!"

"You know — Becky Marwick," I said, pouring myself another glass of Dr Pepper. "She's a freshman. Cute, with real-short blonde hair?"

"And Tony J. is probably Tony Jamison. A junior — tall, thin, buck teeth? He's always on the honor roll," said Kate.

"Oh, sure — sort of a dweeb," said Stephanie. "You think she likes *him*?"

"Maybe," Kate said. "Patti, want more fudge?"

"Thanks," Patti said, taking another piece and chewing it thoughtfully.

58

We lay there on Kate's floor, chowing down and listening to a few more requests. Then Rockin' Ralphie announced, "Time for the WBRM Bulletin Board."

"No, we want music!" Stephanie said firmly, reaching for the tuning knob on the radio.

"Wait a second," said Kate. "I want to hear if there's a movie at the library this weekend." Sometimes on Sunday afternoons the Riverhurst Library shows old silents or foreign movies. One of Kate's favorites is fifty years old, three and a half hours long, in black and white, and all the actors speak Russian!

"He-e-ere we go!" Rockin' Ralphie said. "There's a dance at the Dannerville High School gym next Friday night, tickets two dollars for singles, three dollars for couples, to raise money for the senior trip. The music's by Paul Zot and the Zeros, so *be there*, guys and gals!

"Oka-a-ay," Rockin' Ralphie went on. "And if dancing the night away doesn't get you in shape, The Hampton Ten-Miler will be held on Saturday, the sixteenth, starting at nine o'clock, nine A.M., at the Hampton Town Hall. It's sponsored by the Rotarians, and they're having a big barbecue and flea market at the finish line on Route 25."

59

"Is Roger running, Lauren?" Stephanie asked me.

"He's planning to," I said. Roger has run in a couple of marathons already this year.

"Maybe we should go watch him," Stephanie said glumly. "Nothing better to do on my birthday."

"Sssh!" Kate ordered.

"At the Riverhurst Free Library . . . ," Ralphie was saying. "This Sunday at two o'clock, one show-ing of the 1917 D. C. Griswold production, *Perils of the Storm*. Take your Walkmans and make your *own* sound tracks, rock 'n' rollers," Ralphie added, "be-cause this one is totally si-i-i-*lent*, two and a half hours worth."

"Great!" said Kate. "I've only seen pieces of it on TV — I've never seen the whole thing!"

I sighed thankfully — I already had an excuse lined up. On Saturday my whole family was going to visit my Grandmother Hunter in Bellvale for the weekend. Kate wouldn't be able to rope me into sitting through the movie with her.

"Bear with me, folks — just one more item and we'll be back to the music. This Sunday afternoon's meeting of the Quarks Club is postponed. Members should phone the office to find out when it will be rescheduled . . . *Quarks Club,*" Rockin' Ralphie repeated with a chuckle. "Do you suppose it's a club for ducks? You know — *quark, quark, quark!*"

Stephanie giggled, and Kate switched off the radio.

"What does that word mean, anyway?" I said. It was the second time it had popped up in one day, and I didn't have a clue.

"You're asking me?" Stephanie said.

Kate shrugged. "It sounds made up. Do you know, Patti?" she asked.

Patti was stroking Fredericka, and she didn't even look up. "No idea," she murmured.

"It's time to play . . . Truth or Dare!" said Stephanie.

Chapter 7

Truth or Dare. Stephanie was about to use the Secret Weapon to uncover the truth about Jeff, but Patti didn't look nervous. At least, not any more nervous than any of us do when we're playing Truth or Dare. It can get pretty hairy when you're choosing between a guaranteed-to-be-embarrassing truth and a possibly even more embarrassing dare!

"I'll go first," said Kate.

"I suggested it!" Stephanie complained. I could tell she wanted to get started on Patti right away. But Kate raised an eyebrow at her and she quieted down. After all, we didn't want to be totally obvious about it.

The four of us were sitting in a circle on

Kate's floor. Kate looked at Patti, Stephanie, and me for a second or two with a shrewd smile on her face. Finally she said, "Stephanie — truth or dare?"

"Why not live dangerously?" Stephanie said. "Dare."

"Call Donald Foster!" Kate said gleefully.

"Donald Foster! Ah, come on, Kate — can I change my mind?" Stephanie groaned. "I'll tell you anything you want to know. I'll even tell you how much I weigh this week!" Stephanie's weight is always a deep, dark secret.

"Nope — you know the rules," Kate said. "You chose dare — call Donald."

"What am I supposed to say to him?" Stephanie grumbled, climbing to her feet.

"I don't care. That's *your* problem," Kate replied breezily.

Stephanie tried to get out of it one more time. "It's sort of late — I don't want to wake the Fosters up."

Kate stood up to look out her bedroom window at the Fosters' house and shook her head. "Practically every light is on — you're not going to wake anybody up over there."

"Oh, all right!" Stephanie muttered. "He's going to think I'm a real dork!"

Kate opened her bedroom door a crack to see if Melissa was hanging around, spying on us. Then she darted out into the hall, grabbed the phone off the table, and carried it inside.

Kate closed the door and handed Stephanie the phone. "Go ahead," she said.

"What's his father's name?" Stephanie asked.

"Lawrence," said Kate.

While Stephanie was talking to information, Kate whispered to Patti and me, "If we're lucky, this will make Donald decide that Stephanie's completely immature, and there's no way he'll go to her party."

I made the thumbs-down sign and grinned. Patti smothered a giggle.

". . . two-six-oh-three?" Stephanie was saying. "Thank you."

She pushed the right buttons and held the phone away from her head so we could all hear it ringing. Once . . . twice. . . . On the third ring, Donald picked it up.

"Hello?" He had lowered his voice to answer the phone, which made Kate and me snicker.

Stephanie waved her hand at us to settle down.

"Hello, Donald Foster?" she said, sort of breathlessly. "This is Wendy Rodwin."

"Wendy Rodwin?" Kate mouthed at Patti and me.

Stephanie grinned and made a face.

Wendy Rodwin is this snobby sixth-grader who tried to get Kate and Stephanie kicked out of the video club, just because they were fifth-graders. They used to imitate how she sounded at the meetings — kind of breathy when she was trying to be cute — and Stephanie had dredged it up on the spur of the moment.

"Wendy Rodwin?" Donald said, his voice cracking a little. He was probably thinking of Chuck Morris, Wendy's boyfriend. Chuck's the star forward of the junior high basketball team, and he's seriously *large*. "What can I do for you, Wendy?" Donald asked cautiously.

"Well . . . uh . . ." Stephanie was trying desperately to think why Wendy Rodwin might possibly be calling Donald Foster, when suddenly there was a *click*! The phone went absolutely dead.

"What happened?" I asked.

"Do you think he hung up on me? Maybe he recognized my voice!" Stephanie wailed.

"He couldn't have," Patti said soothingly. "You sounded exactly like Wendy."

Stephanie jiggled the button — not even a dial tone.

"Maybe Donald fainted at the thought of Chuck Morris finding out he was talking to Wendy," Kate suggested with a smirk.

Then we heard hysterical giggling out in the hall.

"Melissa!" Kate said grimly. She threw open the door, and there was Melissa the Monster, holding the telephone plug in her hand and laughing like crazy.

"Mom!" Kate thundered.

Mrs. Beekman stuck her head out of her bedroom at the other end of the hall. "Melissa — what are you doing up?" she said sternly. "Get to bed, right now!"

"Cheer up, kid," Stephanie whispered to Melissa as she trudged gloomily down the hall. "I owe you a Coke float at Charlie's. You're a life-saver."

"I don't know if that counted," Kate said crossly after we'd closed the door again. She was mad because we weren't going to be able to cross Donald off the birthday list.

"Why not? I called him, didn't I?" Stephanie

said. "Now it's *my* turn. Patti, truth or dare?"

"Truth," Patti said.

Maybe she was afraid if she said dare, Stephanie would make her ask Robert Ellwanger, the biggest dweeb in fifth grade, to the movies. That's been a very popular dare this year.

"Okay," said Stephanie, "who's the cutest guy you know right now? Of any age," she added casually.

Patti sat perfectly still for a minute, and a blush moved across her face from her cheeks to her ears. "Donald Foster, I guess," she said at last.

"Donald Foster!" Stephanie squawked. On the one hand, I'm sure Stephanie was pleased to have one of us — other than Melissa — agree with her about Donald. On the other hand, who could believe Patti's answer after having seen *Jeff*?

Stephanie, Kate, and I all stared at Patti uncertainly. "Are you serious?" Kate said at last.

Patti turned even pinker. "Yes," she replied. "Sorry, Kate."

Nobody lies in Truth or Dare, and Patti didn't look as though she were lying. She just looked embarrassed that she'd had to admit how she felt about Donald Foster.

"The game's not over yet," Stephanie murmured in my ear as I sat back down after grabbing another piece of fudge.

"Ouch!" I said, scrambling onto my knees as soon as I'd sat down. "Something is sticking me. . . ." I dug into the back pocket of my jeans and pulled out a sharp piece of blue plastic.

"What *is* that?" Kate said, and Stephanie and Patti leaned forward to look, too.

In a second I'd realized where it had come from, and I closed my fingers over it. But it was too late. The store guard had forgotten to take back the number when he returned my backpack that afternoon. And Patti had already seen the blue plastic number seven with "Bookloft" stamped on it.

Chapter
8

The Truth and Dare game went on a little while longer, but nobody's heart seemed to be in it. Patti didn't ask any questions about the Bookloft, but after seeing that number, she didn't choose truth again.

We watched a rerun of *Alien Village*, the series about blond mutant children who take over a town. Then we went to bed. Stephanie, Kate, and I were pretty worn out after all our spying, and I guess Patti was tired from trying to keep her secret.

Anyway, I dreamed that Patti's mind had been taken over by an alien who looked and acted like Jenny Carlin, and that Jeff was the leader of a bunch of invaders from outer space. I was sort of glad to get away from it all the next day and drive to Bellvale.

Patti went to the city that weekend, to a conference with her parents and Horace. Stephanie's grandmother came to visit her.

Kate was busy taping a Saturday-afternoon foreign film festival on TV, and then there was the Sunday movie at the library. We talked when I got back on Sunday night, though.

"I read the list to Mr. Green over the phone today," Kate told me. "I took David Degan and Pete Stone off, and added Bobby Krieger and Tommy Brown. Mrs. Green will start calling everybody tomorrow."

"What about Donald?" I asked.

"He's on. He'll be invited," she said with a sigh.

Kate, Stephanie, Patti, and I rode our bikes to school together and back on Monday. I told Patti who was on the final guest list for the party on Saturday, while Kate and Stephanie were gabbing. On Tuesday afternoon, all four of us went to Charlie's for our regulars: Kate always gets a Coke float with two scoops of vanilla ice-cream, Stephanie a chocolate shake, Patti a lime freeze, and I get a banana smoothie. On Wednesday, though, Patti started acting lurky again.

At lunch in the cafeteria, Stephanie suggested,

"Let's go to Russell's after school and order the ice-cream cake for Friday night." Russell's makes their deliveries in a cute little blue-and-white truck.

"I love to go to Russell's," I said. "It smells better than any place else in town, except maybe Sweet Stuff." Sweet Stuff is a candy store at the mall that hand-dips its own chocolates.

"Sure — I'll go," said Kate.

Patti shook her head real fast and looked down at her plate. "Uh . . . sorry," she said. "I have to . . . to — "

"It doesn't matter," Kate interrupted sharply. I think we were all getting tired of Patti's big secret about Jeff, especially since we knew it anyway. "The three of us will go."

Patti didn't open her mouth for the rest of the meal. When the final bell rang that afternoon, and we left the building together, all she said was, "Bye — see you tomorrow," kind of weakly.

Kate and Stephanie and I just looked at each other and shrugged as she walked away. "All for one and one for all?" Stephanie said softly, tugging on that curl at the back of her neck.

"I'm beginning to wonder if *Patti* should be on the birthday list!" Kate muttered to me.

71

"Should we follow her?" I asked Stephanie at the bike rack.

"Why bother?" Kate answered. "We know where she's going."

"Yeah — let's check out Russell's. They've started making terrific raspberry turnovers," Stephanie said.

Russell's is way out near the end of Settlers Way, not far from the Riverhurst Wildlife Refuge. It took a while to get there. But it didn't take any time at all to decide what combination of ice cream we wanted in the cake: red, black, and white, or as close as Russell's could get it — strawberry, chocolate fudge, and vanilla.

"With white frosting and chocolate sprinkles, don't you think?" Stephanie said to Kate and me.

"Sounds good," I said.

"Nana gave me twenty dollars before she left on Sunday," Stephanie told us. "I'll treat us to turnovers."

She bought raspberry turnovers at Russell's, and we stopped for Dr Peppers at a little deli across the street.

"Where do you want to eat these?" Kate asked.

"Why don't we go to the Refuge?" I suggested.

"They have those benches near the gate. We can feed the swans."

I like the Wildlife Refuge because it looks as though it hasn't changed in a hundred years. The entrance is a handmade wooden gate with a box attached to it. You drop a quarter into a slot in the box — nobody cheats — push open the gate, and walk past a huge cage for wild animals that have been hurt and are being taken care of by the people at the refuge.

Then there's a cleared space under some oak trees, with benches made of branches and twigs. Beyond that is one end of Munn's Pond, which is always crowded with geese and ducks and swans. The Pond and the Refuge stretch back for miles into a forest.

There was only one car, and a minivan, in the parking lot that afternoon. We locked our bikes to the fence, dropped our quarters into the box, and stepped through the wooden gate. We stopped for a second to look at an owl with a splint on its wing and a raccoon with a broken leg. Then we walked over to the benches and sat down.

Two greedy geese waddled over to us, along with a huge swan we named Rambo because he was so pushy. Kate and Stephanie and I ate a turnover each. They were fantastic! Then we tore up the fourth into little pieces and threw the pieces to the birds.

We were laughing at Rambo, who was arguing with the geese over the food, when Stephanie said, "Somebody's coming."

All three of us looked out at the pond. We could hear splashing noises from over that way and they were getting closer. Then who should appear, wading along the edge of the water, but *Jeff*! And right behind him? You guessed it — *Patti Jenkins*!

Patti froze, and so did we, sort of half-standing, half-sitting. Before anybody could say a word, though, Patti whirled around. She dashed through the trees and out of sight!

"Patti!" Jeff called out. He was wearing a dark gray sweater and faded jeans and looking gorgeous. He stood still for a minute, then he started after her.

"Let's get out of here!" Kate said angrily.

"Right!" said Stephanie. "If Patti doesn't want to see us, we certainly don't want to see her!"

"Either she feels really silly," I said as we hurried toward the gate. "Or. . . ."

"Or she didn't want to introduce us to her precious Jeff!" said Stephanie. "She didn't want him to have to meet her little fifth-grade pals!"

Kate and Stephanie stormed ahead through the gate, and we unlocked our bikes and tore away. All I could think of was, Is this the end of the Sleepover Friends?

Chapter
9

As Stephanie said, *we* hadn't done anything —
it was up to Patti to make the first move. But Patti
didn't call any of us that evening, so we didn't call
her.

Waiting on the corner of Pine and Hillcrest the
next morning before school, Kate and I weren't sure
whether or not Patti would show up. And we couldn't
imagine what we'd say if she did.

"She's got plenty of explaining to do." Kate
looked at her watch. "It's eight twenty-five," she
said. "We're going to be late if we don't leave pretty
soon. Where's Stephanie?"

About thirty seconds later, Stephanie pedaled

around the curve in Pine Street. "Let's go," she said, hardly slowing down.

"What about Patti?" I asked, glancing up Hillcrest — Patti's turn-off on Mill Road.

Stephanie shook her head. "Her mother called my mother a while ago. That's why I'm late."

"And?" said Kate. "Her mother's driving her to school, so she won't have to ride with us?"

"No — Mrs. Jenkins told my mom that Patti had a terrible cold, a slight fever, and that she'd lost her voice." Stephanie said. She glanced sideways at us as we coasted down Hillcrest toward Riverhurst Elementary. "You know how sometimes you can make yourself sick, because you feel bad about something you've done? I think that's probably what's happened to Patti."

That didn't make *me* feel any better. I didn't want Patti to be sick. I wanted all of us to be friends again, and I know Kate and Stephanie did, too.

The three of us moped around school that day, and after school we decided to mope around Stephanie's house.

"Why don't you come over?" she'd suggested when the final bell rang. "Maybe Mom has some more news from the Jenkinses."

But Mrs. Green hadn't heard anything more from Patti's mom. We grabbed some peanut-butter-chocolate-chip cookies and went outside to see how the new wing was going.

It was big, probably as long as my house is wide, but only one story, like the rest of the Greens' house. One wall was in place, and upright boards stood in lines on the concrete foundation.

"The baby's room will be on the left, next to Mom and Dad's bedroom," Stephanie said. "The playroom will be on the right, and there'll be a bathroom in between."

"Lots of space," said Kate.

"Yeah — enough for two or three *more* babies," Stephanie said darkly.

"Do you have a clue about your birthday present?" I asked her.

"Present?" Stephanie said, making a face. "The only presents on Mom and Dad's mind are baby presents, and the only party they care about is a baby shower. Let's check out Dad's office."

We walked around the wing to the backyard.

"Wow — it's neat-looking!" Kate said.

"They did it so fast!" I added.

The walls were all up, with square pieces cut

into the plywood for windows and a rectangular space for a door. The roof was already on, too, with a high peak, and a little skylight on one side. It looked like a tiny little house.

"Isn't it cute?" Stephanie said, leading us inside. "This is the main room, and this little space will be a bathroom, and over there against the side wall Dad's going to have a small refrigerator and a sink."

"Hey!" somebody called from outside.

Stephanie stuck her head through a window hole. "Hey, Walter," she said.

"I saw you yesterday," we heard Walter announce in his squeaky voice. "At the Refuge."

"You were there, too?" Stephanie exclaimed.

"Sure," Walter said.

"He was following Patti again! Let's get him to tell us what went on after we left!" Kate said, rushing out of Mr. Green's office.

Walter Williams was hanging over Stephanie's back fence, his brown glasses sliding down his nose. "Hi," he said when he saw all three of us. "Hi, Lauren," he added, especially for me. Boy, did I feel lucky.

"You were at the Pond?" Kate said.

"With Patti and Jeff?" Stephanie added.

"Jeff?" Walter said, puzzled.

"Walter, I'm sure you've seen Jeff," I said with a friendly smile. Okay, the kid's a genius, but he's only seven and a half. "The tall man with brown hair and a tan?"

"Oh." Walter nodded. "That's Mr. Murdock."

"Mr. Murdock," Stephanie repeated.

"Our teacher," Walter added helpfully.

"Your teacher?" said Kate. "I thought your teacher was Mr. Civello, in 4A."

"Oh — he is," said Walter. "But Mr. Murdock is one of the teachers we have for the Quarks Club."

"*The Quarks Club?*" Kate and Stephanie and I exclaimed.

"Yeah — it just started last week. We're having a lot of extra meetings right now to get organized. There are ten of us in it. Me and Todd Farrell and Betsy Chalfin" — Betsy and Todd are fifth-graders — "and Emily Brady" — a fourth-grader, like Walter — "and Kerry Garvey and Elizabeth Chan and Dana Rice" — sixth-graders — "and — "

"And Patti?" Stephanie interrupted.

"Right," Walter nodded, and his glasses bounced up and down.

"What kind of club is it, Walter?" Kate asked. Which is exactly what I wanted to know — I couldn't think of a more mixed-up group.

"A science club!" said Walter, looking at us as though he thought we were awfully slow to catch on. "You have to be terrific in science to belong. . . ."

"A science club. . . ," said Stephanie.

"That's probably what Mrs. Mead was talking to Patti about after school last week," I said.

"And Mr. Murdock?" said Kate.

"He's a graduate student at the University. Riverhurst Elementary has this arrangement with the science department," Walter said importantly. "His specialty is botany. That's what we were doing at the Pond — collecting water plants. Last Friday we went to the hospital with Miss Sayres, the other teacher."

Aha! No wonder Patti had smelled like a doctor.

Then, changing the subject, Walter asked, "Whose house is this going to be?"

"It's my dad's home office," Stephanie said. "We have to go now, Walter. Bye."

Kate and I followed as Stephanie took off toward our bikes.

"Where are we going?" I asked.

"Patti's," said Stephanie. "We're clearing this up, right now!"

Patti's dad answered the door when we knocked.

"Hi, Mr. Jenkins," Stephanie said. "We came to see how Patti is doing."

"Come in, come in," he said with a big smile. "You may be just what the doctor ordered. Patti — company!" Mr. Jenkins called up the stairs.

"We're coming up!" Stephanie shouted.

The Jenkinses' house is an old wood and stone two-story. Patti's bedroom is small and cozy, with floor-to-ceiling bookshelves crammed with books, stuffed animals, and figurines from all over the world. Patti was lying in the middle of her double bed with the quilt her grandmother had made pulled up to her chin. Billy, the stuffed bear she got on her third birthday, was propped up on the pillow next to her. Her kitten, Adelaide, was snoozing at her feet.

"Now you can't run away," Kate said, grinning at Patti.

"We know about the Quarks Club," Stephanie announced.

"How did you find out?" Patti croaked. She sounded awful, and her nose was bright red from blowing.

"Walter Williams," I said. "Why didn't you tell us about it?"

"Because . . . because I was afraid you'd think I was a total geek," Patti replied in a hoarse whisper. "Like Karla Stamos or Tony Jamison or Walter. And you'd decide I wasn't right for a Sleepover Friend."

"Patti, it's not news to us that you're smart," Kate pointed out. "You're probably the smartest kid in fifth grade, but being smart doesn't have anything to do with being a geek — look at Robert Ellwanger."

All of us giggled. Robert is definitely one of the biggest geeks around, and he's not exactly a shining light as far as schoolwork goes.

"And since you wouldn't tell us about the Quarks," I said, "we imagined all kinds of things."

"Like what?" Patti asked. Her voice was a little stronger.

"Like you had a crush on Jeff," Stephanie said.

"Mr. Murdock," said Kate. "And that you were more interested in chasing him around than doing things with us."

"Oh, no!" Patti started giggling again, which

made her sneeze. "He's a *teacher*! Besides, he's engaged."

"To a blonde girl who looks like a model?" I asked.

Patti nodded and blew her nose.

"We saw them kissing from the window of the Bookloft," Kate said.

"We were following you, trying to figure out if you were going to dump us," Stephanie told her.

"I'd never do that," Patti said, suddenly serious, "not in a million years. The Quarks' meetings are only going to be once a week after tomorrow, but still, I'd give them up in a minute if there was a chance it would mess *us* up!"

"No way that's going to happen," said Stephanie firmly.

"I just wish I could be in the Quarks *and* be a good Sleepover Friend," Patti said.

"No reason you can't," I said. "Right?" I asked the others.

"Right!" Kate and Stephanie agreed.

Chapter 10

On Friday morning, everything was back to normal. Patti's cold was a lot better, so we all rode to school together. That afternoon, she and the other Quarks visited Arista Laboratories, where they make flavors for foods. Kate had to run some errands with her mother, and I jogged a few miles with Roger. But we all arrived at Stephanie's at seven-thirty sharp that evening.

Russell's had delivered the red, white, and black ice-cream cake, and Patti brought some red birthday candles from home. We had our own party in Stephanie's bedroom, and she opened our present then.

She loved the jumper, and it looked really great

on her. "At least you guys remembered my birthday," she said, looking at herself in the mirror and practicing her Brooke Shields smile.

We stayed up really late watching a double-feature on *Chiller Theater* — Patti and I both hate scary movies, but in honor of Stephanie's birthday, we sat through both without complaining. And we slept late the next morning.

When we finally got up, Stephanie's parents had a blueberry-pancake breakfast waiting for us. And there was a tiny silver package tied with red ribbon sitting next to Stephanie's plate.

"Happy birthday, honey," Mr. Green said, giving Stephanie a big hug.

"We hope you like it," Mrs. Green added, giving her a kiss.

"I bet it's jewelry!" Stephanie said, undoing the ribbon. "The ring we saw in Bunty's last weekend, right, Mom?"

When she pulled off the paper and opened the box, what she found instead was a regular brass key.

"A key. . . ," said Stephanie, looking at her parents. "A key?"

"To the door. . . ," her mother began.

" . . . of the little house in back!" her father finished.

"Your office?" said Stephanie, not understanding at all.

"No, sweetie — it's *yours!*" said her dad. "We thought, with the baby coming, you'd like a place to get away from it all once in a while."

"Your father's office is going to be in the addition — what we've been calling the playroom," her mother added.

Wow! As an only child, Stephanie's always had a lot of extras, but this was pretty amazing. It looked to me as though her parents were maybe going a little overboard, to make sure Stephanie wouldn't feel neglected — and think the kinds of things she's been thinking — with the new baby coming. But it was a great present, and it was definitely making Stephanie happy.

"A place we can hang out, play music as loud as we want — we can even have sleepovers out there! How perfect!" Stephanie shrieked.

She gave both of her parents a giant hug and jumped up and down. "My *own apartment!*"

"Not quite," Mrs. Green said, laughing. "I realize you're eleven now, but we're not exactly ready to have you leave home yet. It's just a sort of extra-private playroom — a grown-up playhouse."

"We'll have to start looking for curtains, and some chairs, and maybe a table, and . . . everything!" Stephanie said to us.

"I thought we might drive to the mall early this afternoon," Mrs. Green said. "Get some decorating ideas."

Mr. Green winked at Kate and Patti and me.

That's how we ended up at the Pizza Palace at two o'clock without tipping Stephanie off. When we opened the door and all the kids yelled "Surprise!" Stephanie was absolutely speechless —for the first time in her life.

Jane Sykes, Sally Mason, Erin Wilson, Robin Becker, Tracy Osner, Mark Freedman, Larry Jackson, Michael Pastore, Henry Larkin, Alan Reese. . . .

"Donald's here!" I said to Kate.

He was standing in the middle of a circle of admiring girls, smoothing down his blond hair and flashing a glossy smile.

"Ick!" I said.

"If you were going to keep a secret, that's the

secret you should have kept," Kate said to Patti.

"What secret?" Patti asked.

"That Donald Foster is the cutest guy you know," Kate said with a grin.

Sleepover Friends forever!

SLEEPOVER FRIENDS

#14 Lauren Takes Charge

Stephanie turned her attention to me again. "Lauren, you ought to be getting more privileges out of this, at least. You'll be doing a lot of adult-type stuff around your house with your mom away at her new job all day long."

I shook my head — I hadn't thought anything through, of course.

"Now's the time to negotiate. . . . If you wait too long, your parents will start taking all of your extra work for granted," Stephanie said.

"Extra work?" I said.

"Sure, like fixing dinner, and you'll probably have to clean up the house during the week, and maybe even do some laundry. . . ."

Clean the house? I was thinking. I can't even keep my own room clean.

Win the sleeping bag of your dreams!

Enter the
SLEEPOVER FRIENDS
SLEEPING BAG GIVEAWAY!

50 WINNERS!

Your sleepover party won't be complete without a Sleepover Friends sleeping bag! Now you can enter the Sleepover Friends Giveaway and win a roomy (28″ x 57″), comfy sleeping bag! All you have to do is complete the coupon below and return by October 31, 1989.

This soft, plush sleeping bag is pink and has an adorable white sheep pattern on the inside. It is washable, has a heavy-duty zipper, and elastic straps that make it easy to roll up and compact to carry. Bring it to your next sleepover party and have the best time ever! Kate, Lauren, Stephanie, and Patti always have a great party in their series packed with fun and adventure—the **Sleepover Friends!**

Rules: Entries must be postmarked by October 31, 1989. Contestants must be between the ages of 7 and 12. Winners will be picked at random from all eligible entries received. No purchase necessary. Valid only in the U.S.A. Employees of Scholastic Inc., affiliates, subsidiaries, and their families are not eligible. Void where prohibited. Winners will be notified by mail.

Fill in your name, age, and address below or write the information on a 3″ x 5″ piece of paper and mail to: SLEEPOVER FRIENDS GIVEAWAY, Scholastic Inc., P.O. Box 673, Cooper Station, New York, NY 10276.

Sleepover Friends Sleeping Bag Giveaway

Where did you buy this Sleepover Friends book?

☐ Bookstore   ☐ Drug Store   ☐ Supermarket

☐ Discount Store   ☐ Book Club   ☐ Book Fair

☐ Other _____
       specify

Name _____

Birthday_____ Age _____

Street _____

City, State, Zip _____

SLE1288

Pack your bags for fun and adventure with

SLEEPOVER FRIENDS™
by Susan Saunders

Join Kate, Lauren, Stephanie and Patti at their great sleepover parties every weekend. Truth or Dare, scary movies, late-night boy talk—it's all part of **Sleepover Friends!**

☐ MF40641-8	#1 Patti's Luck	$2.50
☐ MF40642-6	#2 Starring Stephanie	$2.50
☐ MF40643-4	#3 Kate's Surprise	$2.50
☐ MF40644-2	#4 Patti's New Look	$2.50
☐ MF41336-8	#5 Lauren's Big Mix-Up	$2.50
☐ MF41337-6	#6 Kate's Camp-Out	$2.50
☐ MF41694-4	#7 Stephanie Strikes Back	$2.50
☐ MF41695-2	#8 Lauren's Treasure	$2.50
☐ MF41696-0	#9 No More Sleepovers, Patti?	$2.50
☐ MF41697-9	#10 Lauren's Sleepover Exchange	$2.50
☐ MF41845-9	#11 Stephanie's Family Secret	$2.50
☐ MF41846-7	#12 Kate's Sleepover Disaster	$2.50
☐ MF42301-0	#13 Patti's Secret Wish	$2.50
☐ MF42300-2	#14 Lauren Takes Charge (July '89)	$2.50
☐ MF42299-5	#15 Stephanie's Big Story (August '89)	$2.50
☐ MF42662-1	Sleepover Friends' Super Guide (August '89)	$2.50

PREFIX CODE 0-590-

Available wherever you buy books...or use the coupon below.

Scholastic Inc. P.O. Box 7502, 2932 E. McCarty Street, Jefferson City, MO 65102

Please send me the books I have checked above. I am enclosing $_____

(Please add $1.00 to cover shipping and handling). Send check or money order—no cash or C.O.D.'s please

Name _____

Address _____

City _____ State/Zip _____

Please allow four to six weeks for delivery. Offer good in U.S.A. only. Sorry, mail order not available to residents of Canada. Prices subject to change.

SLE1288